trapped in a thought

trapped in a thought

mahi pandya

First published by
Papertowns Publishers
72, Vishwanath Dham Colony,
Niwaru Road, Jhotwara,
Jaipur, 302012

Trapped in A Thought

ISBN Print Book - 978-93-87131-30-9

For my family and friends
thank you for being there, reading my poems
and most of all tolerating me.

CONTENTS

Tales of Woe

Poetry and Darkness

Those We Adore and Care For

Existence and Infancy

TALES OF WOE

DOUBT

All those remarks, the looks of confusion,
What were those reassuring words, were they an illusion?
Now I question, have I disappointed everyone?
What's my crime, what have I done?

It's not their fault, maybe I'm the problem,
These are my battles, they can't fight them.
I try so hard to find the motivation,
But uncertainty has attacked my resolution.

Worthless, good for nothing, these words can kill,
My heart is empty, a void only love can fill.
Oblivious to all my efforts, they stare,
They won't even try to understand, how is that fair?

The canopy of blame, that hides the sunlight,
I won't grow into a tree, even if I fight.
I'm underwater and the chains of doubt have held me down,
Pull me up with a little love, don't let me drown.

MAHI PANDYA

TIRED OF REALITY

Take me down with you,
I'm clueless and lost without my crew.
I'm ready to be consumed,
Questioning my life decisions, what if I'm doomed.

It's a pain to be here, to breathe,
I wanna dig six feet deep in the ground and lay underneath.
My lungs are fatigued, tired of the monotone,
The soil will change my spirit just like a seed that was sown.

But alas, you're here and so am I
You will smile one day and those tears will dry.
Don't worry, it'll get better, let's hope,
But not unless you cut loose from that metal rope.

The one that entraps your beating heart,
Let that heart pump, let this be a start.
It suffocates your dreams, they choke, they grasp for air,
If you stick around there might be a Dream we could share.

Meaningless words that don't cost a dime,
Words that are confessions of desires and every crime.
But we're tired, oh so tired of the chase,
Cause the truth is if we stop, the reality is too hard to face.

MAHI PANDYA

OUTSIDE THIS BEDROOM

I search for answers of questions never asked before,
I've created my own hell behind my bedroom door.
These questions are truly horrifying,
But somehow I'm drawn to them without trying.

That little bed with colourful sheets,
This is where my body and soul meets.
I think about the future as I lay on the bed,
I think about when and why will I be dead.

I shouldn't be thinking of death, I'm way too young,
But outside this room are vultures, they have no control
over their tongue.
They wanna lure me out to put me down with words,
And I'm too afraid to face these scary birds.

I stayed outside this room for years,
But now I'm tired of the constant hurt and tears.
I'll lock the door and be buried under those questions,
I've stopped hearing condolences, stopped taking
suggestions.

They say I've lost all purpose and productivity,
But they don't care that I lost my peace of mind, my sanity.
I write these words, these words are my tomb,
Cause someday I have to face the world outside this
bedroom.

MAHI PANDYA

ACCEPTED

I admit I'm less than perfect
Maybe an accident, a side effect
The ones that see me wanna look away
And I hide in the night, in the shadows of the day

I've wished for normality time and again
And every word said to me is garnished with disdain
I'm sorry I wanna tell them
I'm sorry for being the root of their every problem

I laugh at myself so others don't have to
That doesn't mean what I say, isn't true
Maybe I'm dead weight on the surface on earth
So why am I here? I question my birth

One day I'll relieve them of my existence
And I'll hold the anger in till I lose all my patience
I'm clueless but maybe my time has started
And just maybe one day I'll be accepted.

MAHI PANDYA

MIDNIGHT SAGA

The nights lure me in with peacefulness,
swallow me completely,
My mind refuses to rest but my eyes are tired and dull,
almost sleepy.
Every night there's a different villan that I find.
And all of them just want one thing, my peace of mind.

The poetry that forms in my head.
They are birthed by tears I shed
From the depths of darkness, the trench of trauma,
The problems that keep me awake, it isn't just drama.

I've realized now that the monsters are in my mind,
not under my bed
They attack the darkest part of me, they want me dead.
As I watch the sunrise, my darkness dies away.
But they will come back at night, after another day.

MAHI PANDYA

HATER

I don't want to be negative,
But the concept of hate is relative.
Talk about that passive aggressive passion,
They wear a frown everyday like its fashion.

Why investigate these feelings of anger,
When life is just one big cliff-hanger?
How do you look past their discretion?
You need therapy? Let's have a session.

Listen to the words you're spitting,
That's my last nerve you keep hitting.
But one day it will explode,
And I won't be able to take the load.

I kept those thoughts under closed doors,
Kept the waves of insults away from the shore.
But one day my deepest inhibitions will falter,
And I too will become a hater.

MAHI PANDYA

DISTRACTIONS

Whisk me away to the land of rainbows,
Where it's all simple like the TV shows.
The puffs of smoke form different shapes,
Rolled up joints and bubblegum vapes.

My Mind is foggy, my vision is a blur,
My tears keep dripping and my words slur.
Maybe I'll throw up but I can't digest reality,
I need a hit to calm my nerves, kick out the anxiety.

Tequila tastes awful and vodka burns my tongue,
But now this feels normal and nothing' wrong.
Every other day I'm exhausted of this spiral,
But then reality hits and I embrace denial.

Who even thinks about consequences and tomorrows,
When I'm shattering under the tower of sorrows.
I know I need to find a path and take action,
I need purpose and goals not another distraction.

MAHI PANDYA

CONTROL

I like to know about the future
I ain't a psychic so not knowing is torture
I need to know about what everyone thinks
I'm not a mind reader so that stinks

A day without a plan and I lose my mind
I need to think ahead, I hate being left behind
I'm not a neat freak but no one can touch my mess
I decide for myself, hate being helpless

I won't give my opinions but don't try changing me
I want to know what will happen and who I will be
I will try too much or not try at all
I will always stand still, not ready for the fall

Don't go telling me I'm perfect,
My defence is on an alert, always erect
Maybe I'm hopeless, I have a damaged soul
Maybe this is OCD, but I love being in control

MAHI PANDYA

IGNORANCE

When you keep your eyes on the ground,
You miss the mass of bodies running around,
When you smile at something,
You miss sorrow in the song that she sings.

If you sulk in your own misery,
You'll miss the good times, you must hurry.
If you keep adorning your own body,
You'll never be grateful, never feel sorry

If you lock yourself in your room
You won't be able to live, it'll be your doom.
Let others bring you down, and you've lost already
If you see the world you'll see not everyone is greedy.

So stop being naive, drop the act of innocence.
Clear your head and you can make a difference.
The light of hope may blind you,
But ignorance is a curse, it can bind you.

MAHI PANDYA

POETRY AND DARKNESS

DARK

Last night I sat in the dark
But could hear the traffic hum, the dogs bark
I never sat in the dark before
Usually, I have a night light and an open door

All the darkness was so new, but it felt old
It was endless, I kept falling, nothing to hold
Why does it scare me but why do I love it
There were no compartments and I just fit

I couldn't see my face, couldn't stare at the mirror
I felt the warmth of the night and embraced the horror
The darkness around merged with the one inside me
Not restricted to a solid form, I was fluid, I was free

And then the stillness enveloped me, whole
There were no barriers between me and my soul
That night stole my trauma, my pain
I'm addicted, can't wait to sit in the dark again.

MAHI PANDYA

POETRY IN THE DARK

I reached into my darkness, found the thought,
Swam in dangerous waters, amongst the creatures I fought.
Promised myself, I'd never go there again,
But if it gets me a few rhymed words, then it wasn't in vain.
To you it's great poetry, it's art.
To me it's my nightmares, the evil of my heart.
Cause these words on paper, they keep me alive,
I've been cruising the edge and now I dive.
Falling straight down, to oblivion I suppose,
These words describe my life, the path I chose.
If you read into it to try and save me, you'll fail.
It's all useless now, that ship has already set sail.
I am content too, I am happy,
But when the curtain falls, you'll find me.
It'll pass they say, I hope they're right,
Cause like in the movies the dark cannot win and
I will fight.

MAHI PANDYA

FATE?

They ask me why I write about pain and agony
They won't believe my words, call them phoney
They tell me, I've not experienced real trauma
What can I say, guess I was born with it, it's not drama

They say I'm not sad, I'm happy and kind
But there's a pool of sadness in my mind,
It drains me, at the same time quenches my thoughts
And it's scary to actually think all the things I fought

All these metaphors, I wish I was direct
I wish I was decisive why can't I just select
I want to choose the life I want, I want my pick
I want it to end, put my mind at ease quick

All these poems, I can write a Bible
It's my last supper, I've taken a seat on the table
Trust issues, I think all love has undertones of hate.
I've heard what they say, but I believe poetry is my fate.

MAHI PANDYA

INK

My words seem limited now,
And I sit back and think, wow.
How the times have changed,
My thoughts are old but I've not aged.

How can a tiny brain fit so much,
Useless overthinking and nothing important as such.
Secrets I can't tell anyone are all hidden here,
I broadcast these lines with nothing to fear.

I'm so in love with this art,
Sometimes I kill myself and hurt my heart.
New ideas and exciting feelings,
I don't need to feel them anymore just write things.

I can't even stop now, it's too late,
But what will I do with this feelings of hate.
Let me go, let me breathe,
Stop gnawing at my brain with sharp teeth.

Sometimes I wish to be normal,
Sometimes I wish i wasn't moral.
Nothing to say so I just blink,
What I want to say is said in ink.

MAHI PANDYA

DOWNHILL

I Say it's a downhill battle
And with every win the ground will rattle
I even gained a lot of speed
Who knew Speed breakers will become a need

It's not even weird anymore,this happens every day
My eyes are closed and down is the only way
Their hate is pulling me, pain acting like gravity
They don't even think twice, they don't even have pity

I've turned around now,I've opened my eyes
And the way up is much harder, it's surrounded with lies
I've lost all my speed and I'm slow as a snail
And they're still pulling me, they want to see me fail

I'm fighting against the agony its tempting me
I want to let the slope control me
They say let things be as they are
If I do so, I'm going be stuck here, and I'll never go far

MAHI PANDYA

WHY DO I WRITE?

When I write, words just seem to rhyme,
I can write for you, without even charging a dime.

I write about what I really mean,
My work is very different, unseen.

They say the pen is mightier than the sword,
I can write about dreams, fears, creatures, even the lord.

Poetry is the reason for my happiness,
I write when I'm sad, when my emotions are a mess.

Every syllable I write tells the real story,
I write for revenge, I won't stop even if you're sorry.

I'm too young, my poems are too deep,
But I don't believe in steps, I just take the leap.

They say I'm not talented, I'm no good,
And they keep trying to put me down, spoil my mood.

But I've decided to fight,
And I won't take cheap shots, I won't hit, I'll just write!

MAHI PANDYA

ARTIST

You wonder how my brain works
I'm allowed to be cynical, that's a perk
All my experiences playing in my head,
Almost always thinking about oblivion and being dead

My community is insane don't question it
All of us outsiders, we will never fit
My brain, keeping my mind caged
All the happiness you see is mostly staged

Can't understand me? so you ask for an explanation
I attract pain, trauma peeks my fascination
Egoistic and cryptic, they describe me like that
So much self doubt, I even question facts.

The more I resist the more it grows
I can try to hide it but it will show
The art in my veins, will flow when I bleed
Not a hobby or profession, actually it's a need.

I don't know how this started or if I'm any good
Me and my kind are unreliable, shifting moods.
We don't give up, hang on the tightest.
Guess that makes me a lunatic, an artist.

MAHI PANDYA

ALL KINDS OF ME

A tight ponytail,
Converse shoes.
Hope in my eyes that I won't fail,
Sure that I can resolve my own issues.
Little black dress,
Heels, the height of a tower.
Let you know my body is no object you can caress.
Let you know who has the power.
Ripped jeans,
Flip flops for my feet.
Sure can say no and show you what it means,
I can dance on my own, can feel the beat.
In my underwear,
Or in nothing at all.
Still can take care of my own,
And pick myself up when I fall.

MAHI PANDYA

REPAIRED

Most of my life I've been incomplete,
I've given up now, accepted defeat.
But every other day I'm inspired,
Something infuriates me, and I stop being tired.

Those days are like dreams,
And it's confusing that it's not what it seems.
I question everything about myself, self worth,
Question my purpose, my birth.

And I ruin my self for art,
Cause I'm numb, I have a stone heart.
This art will take me no where I'll be forever lost,
I'll lay there upon the grass slowly, I'll be covered with frost.

How many people will see through these words?
Cause people follow people in herds.
I keep needing validation, when will I be enough,
I guess I enjoy this challenge, I want it to be tough.

Someday I'll wake up, motivated for real,
I'll sleep through the night, I'll know what I feel.
But right now I'm just a kid, anxious and scared,
And on that morning when I'm well rested, I'll be repaired.

MAHI PANDYA

MISTRESS SLEEP

She has unimaginable control, she's a mistress,
She can get you to deceive, she can get you to confess.
Her eyes are like a maze, look too deep and you're lost.
And you'll fall for her every time without realizing the cost.

She's a sorceress, she's the master of your mind,
She can't be fooled, she knows your kind.
She comes and goes as she pleases, no one tells her anything,
Her voice soft, gentle and for you she'll sing.

She's unattainable by will, but only by worth,
And she'll make you suffer, turn back and forth.
Her spirit can be good or evil depends how you treat her,
When she takes over, your vision will blur.

At some point I must've wronged her, cause she left me here,
I plead for her to come back but she's gone forever, I fear.
Cause I need her to survive, we all do,
She blesses some with her power, there are very few.

Darkness is her best-friend, they never break their bond,
They have magic in them, they don't need a magic wand.
They are witches, witches of the same coven,
For after all this time, I can only assume that sleep is a woman.

MAHI PANDYA

ANXIETY

Some nights are different, they hurt more,
My body runs hot and I lay on the cool floor.
Inside these four walls, I find myself a corner,
And I start sweating as my head gets warmer.

The pain starts in my chest, I hear pounding,
I lose track of my thoughts and my surrounding.
Maybe I'm being punished for having a weak brain,
It's more than I can handle, more than I can contain.

I try everything to distract myself and forget it all in the morning,
And when my eyes moisten, it's just a warning.
It feels like running out of air, like dying,
But it's just me being "over dramatic" and crying.

When anxiety attacks, everything is in vain,
And every morning I pray for it to never happen again.
But let me tell you this, it'll go away,
It's not a permanent disorder, it won't stay.

MAHI PANDYA

SHUT DOWN

I'll stop whatever I'm doing,
stop hearing everything, the applause and the booing.
I'll be just a functioning body on autopilot,
I'll walk the straight line blindly, no room to pivot.

This has happened before and will happen again,
There's no way to go now, all effort is vain.
Hey will I ever learn the drill?
Can I ever just be the best, change by will?

This year, this year is so familiar,
All my moods, my thoughts are so similar.
The same cycle of self sabotage and doubt,
There's no surety, yet I know how this will play out.

Cause friend I'm just trying to warn you,
Hoping you'll be there after what I'll do.
"Yes" you'll say but you won't understand,
You'll want to help me, but you can just hold my hand.

As you sail soft waters, I'll fight my storms,
As you follow rules I'll break the norms.
I wish we could wait till the sky goes brown,
But the time has come, the time for me to shut down.

MAHI PANDYA

THOSE WE ADORE AND CARE FOR

BY MY SIDE

Today I realized how much I've grown,
I recognize the evil in the angels I've known.
It hurt to feel like that again,
I remember why I changed my self, it wasn't in vain.

I want to bang my head into a wall,
If that'll give me a fresh start and forget all.
I know it's foolish to dwell in the past,
Because memories will fade but the lessons will last.

All the feelings come to life when I talk to you,
They keep me up all night, there's nothing I can do.
Toxic, you wanted to poison me to death,
Choking, you were stealing life from me with every breath.

For years I was blindsided and betrayed,
I was too distracted, I should've never stayed.
I realized now, you're too shallow,
I kept denying it, it was a hard pill to swallow.

What's done is done, can't change the past,
I've moved on, I'm free at last.
But every now and then nostalgia hits me like a tide,
But the truth is we were never meant to be,
you don't belong by my side.

MAHI PANDYA

CHANCE

I'll chase you till I drop dead
You're not good to me, I can't get that in my head
You're forbidden fruit I've gotta have you
You look like bliss, but that just ain't true

You control my dreams, showed me you can help me
All the mist has blurred my vision so I just can't see
I wrote my first poetry about you, they thought it was lame
Why do we try controlling you, you can't be tamed

It's been a while since we last met,
Thought I was through with you, I lost that bet
Talked about life and you asked me if I was okay.
Empty promises, you said you'll whisk me away

The lessons I had learned last time, forgotten
Why do I believe that history can be rewritten
I hear them warning me, I hear my calling from above
Its a game of chance, but what if I don't take a chance on love.

MAHI PANDYA

APPEARANCE

I have a question, what's the deal with appearance?
I see everyone the same, what's the difference?
How I dress up decides my character, my kind,
Nobody seems to care about my soul, my mind.

You are the devil, showing off your Prada
You talk about equality, its all just a propaganda
You judge me cause you want to crush my spirit
But actually Your judgement has no merit.

Look around they're doing the same to you,
It's a vicious cycle, tomorrow it'll find someone new.
If I'm not sorry, they want me to have shame
They say they're different but, they're all the same.

I'll colour my lips, but my words will remain black and white.
I might be short but my confidence will have height.
Doesn't matter if I'm a size zero or a plus
For once, Let's look beyond what society has taught us.

MAHI PANDYA

TO THAT BROKEN HEARTED GIRL

She does not miss him
She misses, being wanted.
Right now her eyes look dim
Because her thoughts are haunted.

Nothing makes her feel good,
Her every smile seems fake.
She hides her sadness with food,
No one wants to give, they only take.

He wasn't special at all,
But at least he was there.
He would catch her when she would fall,
And he would listen when she would share.

When they need to laugh they call her,
And she always smiles and comforts everyone.
but if she needs advice they have none to offer,
And if she needs a shoulder to cry on, there isn't one.

"He wasn't right for me" she would say,
She will find someone new, she would think.
But she was still alone, in the middle of the day,
As if 'the one' would appear in a blink.

But what can a girl do except wait,
She knew she won't be alone anymore.
And maybe he's just running late,
But her sailing ship will surely find the shore.

MAHI PANDYA

GLOWING CONCEPT

I've been waiting for it happen, when will this stop?
When will the cornucopia flourish, when will the ball drop?
Is it even real? I wonder.
Maybe they're unfamiliar grounds I'll never ponder.

Questions that haunt my mind, hundreds at a time,
Maybe I'm too wishful, too expectant, is that a crime?
People my age seem to find it easily, so I inquire,
It's not that I need it, my condition is not dire.

I have a purpose, I have goals, I have aimed too high,
But when I stop for a breather, I wish for a hand
to hold me as I cry.
I'm double-sided, I won't let anyone know me,
But I curse myself for being as alone a girl can be.

When I touched the glowing concept it burned,
All my hopes dissipate, and my beliefs turned.
Too young to handle this, so I'll stay here,
watch people take the leap from above,
I'll mourn for myself but won't cry in the name of love.

MAHI PANDYA

ALONE

I know no one here,
my heart is filled with doubt and fear.

It'll be a while before I make friends,
Cause I'm not cool and I don't Know the trends.

This new world is very strange,
To fit in I'll have to change.

It's like a war and I'm fighting alone,
The wounds from the past have opened up,
the rumours have flown.

Now people are mean and their words can kill,
I won't run away I'll sit still.

If I be strong this time and hold my ground,
Maybe people will come around?

MAHI PANDYA

I LOST ALL MY FEELINGS

I guess I'm staying inside today
Maybe a few smiles got lost in the way
I'm stuck in this ditch, flooding up quickly
What to think, what not to think it's tricky

Why do I feel my words aren't enough
Why did I let myself be weak, I should be tough
I have tried to heal this wound alone
Now I'm asking for help I'm not made of stone

Is it weird that I'm moving but going nowhere
I'm seeing the monstrosity, cruelty, but I don't care
You can stab me and I won't bleed
I've lost all feeling, it's time to take heed

You have done this to me, your doubts
I didn't tell you and you never tried to find out
All my emotions are drying up, I'm growing numb
Once so Compassionate, now I'm scared of what
I've become.

MAHI PANDYA

NUDGE

I'm shaking again, I can feel the chill,
I feel different in these shoes I have to fill.
I don't know who I should turn to,
Left everyone behind, what did I do.

Every rhyme is about my cold unfeeling heart,
I've aimed for the bull's eye, just have to throw the dart.
I'll Let my friends speak badly of me,
They're just saying what they see.

I've been stress eating but my weight tells me it's time
Time to give up the self pity and own up to the crime
I'm growing up, learning to recover,
I'm laughing again, singing in the shower.

Let's not dwell in the past,
Let's get up, move on, do something fast.
I'm starting out, all's forgiven, I hold no grudge.
I'm so close to greatness I just need a little nudge.

MAHI PANDYA

EXISTENCE AND INFANCY

CHILDREN FOR A SECOND

When I was eight, everything was right,
Awarded for finishing dinner and punished
for getting into a fight.
There was no grey, everything was either black or white,
And when it was bed time I was out like a light.

Now these mundane days make me choke,
And today I'm reminded of all the promises I broke.
Even though I made them as a joke,
The guilt is overwhelming, and in realization I croak.

Those playdates we used to have don't happen anymore,
Because experiences changed us, we became rotten
to the core.
Even if I try I'll never be like I was before,
I'm exhausted, tired and my body is sore.

I used to dream big, now that feels like a crime,
And I'm so tired of overthinking all the time.
I'm numb inside, the feeling is sublime,
We were children for just a second but adulthood lasts
for lifetime.

MAHI PANDYA

HEY THERE, SWEET CHILD

Hey there sweet child,
Let go, it's okay.
You're young, you're allowed to be wild,
Live in the moment, live for the day.

Maybe you aren't allowed to go crazy,
But don't care about the rules.
Soon your hair will be grey and your vision hazy,
Do your own thing, don't listen to the fools.

Let your hair down, dance and sing,
Act your age, go play on the slides and swings.
Cause once you're grown, there's no going back,
This charm and light you will lack.

It's OK to plan but it's never OK to worry,
You're missing out on life and later you'll be sorry.
Hey there sweet child, it's okay,
Let go, live for the day.

MAHI PANDYA

TEENS

They're hard to understand, complex
Always confused between love and sex
Oh what a travesty this is
They're being distant? It's usually a hit and miss

Don't stress over it, they always come back
You think you're giving advice but to them it's an attack
Maybe not all of them are the same
Maybe not all of them want attention, want fame

Oh how stereotypical of me, I agree
You pamper them too much, they'll want to be free
They say " you can never blame us "
And they will always throw you under the bus

Beware cause they're your future,
They're gonna be wild until they mature
they may be sad and glued to they're screens
But this is they're world, a world for the teens

MAHI PANDYA

SIXTEEN FOREVER

I'm not ten, nor am I twenty yet, I'm stuck in between,
trapped at the awkward age of sixteen.
I'm never high, never low, never in, never out.
Never perfectly still, always scream and shout.

Made too many friends, but only a few that will stick.
Everything gives me anxiety, everything makes me sick.
Clueless as ever, confused as hell .
Pressure to make my parents proud, they taught me well.

Depressed, but it's " just a phase ",
And I'm attacked, consumed by this monster with out a face.
Have to fight him on my own, a battle for sanity,
For I still have a lot to learn about the world, humanity.

Eyes wide open, I never fall asleep,
Thoughts cloud my brain, a little too deep.
Alone with these thoughts, minutes turn into hours....
All this, is reality yours and mine,ours.

MAHI PANDYA

MOTHER

We may fight and shout,
But you are the one I really care about.
I might tell you what your problems are,
All said and done, you are my only star.

I tell you everything I feel,
You share the problems I have to deal.
It's not something we both know,
It's not something we both can show.

How much ever we scream and yell,
Even if I say 'go to hell',
I know you'll be by my side,
These are feelings we involuntarily hide.

You are a masterpiece, unseen,
With my every expression you know exactly what I mean.
You are there to wipe my tears,
You help me fight my fears.

I might be loud, naughty and wild,
You still call me your sweet child.
No one can love me like this, no other,
How much ever we fight you'll always be my mother.

MAHI PANDYA

I WANT TO BE

Today, I want to be good,
Have a conversation without being rude,
I want to be the angel I pray upon,
And stare at the sky laying on a grass lawn.

I want to be someone's greatest accomplishment,
To grow with someone, strive for improvement.
I want to feel the love I once read about.
To be so proud of us, that I need to shout.

Someday I want to prove the world wrong,
I'll fight all my problems and be strong.
I want to see the pride in my parent's eyes.
To feel content when I'm old and wise.

I want to write words that ooze honesty,
I want to be smart and rational, not too hasty.
My poetry should make people feel things,
My poetry could be a song that someone sings.

So many wishes, what will come of them, who knows,
Maybe they'll fade away, turn to nothing but shadows.
It's unnerving to be feel, but now I'm ready,
One day I'll be what I want to be and my heartbeat will
steady.

MAHI PANDYA

DARE TO LIVE

Sometimes, times change,
The known become strange.

The strongest couples, fight and go on a break,
And the realest people in your life become fake.

People talk, rumours start,
Emptiness grows in your heart.

You will feel betrayed cause friends lie,
Soon enough you want to give up, you want to die.

At times like this have faith in humanity,
Talk to someone, act with maturity.

Because who says death will bring peace,
There are still so many opportunities, you have to seize.

Amidst the darkness you can be the light,
Don't give up, push back with all your might.

The future is unknown, you are just unaware,
Life can be all you want, you just have to dare.

MAHI PANDYA

DEAR PEACE

I step out of my mould, so new so naked
Tried something new but I had to fake it
I talked to you, thinking that you'll stay
Guess is pretty clear you don't do what you say

You're ashamed of Me? Well I am too
You've iced me out, well nothing new
This is an exciting game we play
Why do I always apologize, what is this debt I have to repay?

It lasted for a second but I felt you, I thought it was a start
I felt the warmth of my breath, the racing of my heart
You come and go like the wind, unpredictable
Stay here, we can hold each other to be stable

What do I have to do to deserve you
I'm not the best, I'm an okay human at least that's true
I wish i could bribe you but all the money isn't enough
Dear peace, I need you, this life is tough

MAHI PANDYA

SMILE

I appreciate the are you ok's,
They help me on most days.
But today I'm tired, I'm tired of the pain,
Nothing new, I've endured them again and again.

There are questions, that I've not found answers to,
Goals I've not set yet, what am I going to do.
Doubts that they have about me, they hurt,
Usually I keep it to myself but sometimes I blurt.

Now I gotta explain it to the kind souls who care,
But they won't understand even if I'm able to share.
Ones who love me the most have caused this,
Am I one step away from forever darkness or eternal bliss?

When I'm better, maybe you'll read these words,
And I'll run, run away from the herds.
Hide beneath a rock, wait for the layers to settle over me,
And I'll show my face again when I've plastered
a smile for you to see.

MAHI PANDYA

REINVENT

I blackout for a moment,
Think about when I decided to reinvent
It's been a while since I was inspired
Before that I was disinterested and tired

It's like caffeine, keeping me awake
But it's temporary, doesn't last longer than a earthquake
I need you to push me till I break
I need to trust you, tell me you're not a fake

Oh look at that I did something productive,
I didn't cry today, wow, was I being positive?
I love this fire burning inside me,
I wish it would swallow me cause that's how I want to be

Let's congratulate us, we are alive another day
I might not be driven but breathing is awesome anyway
Go ahead procrastinate, you can give up tomorrow
If I need a little hope, can I borrow?

This poem is motivating, isn't it?
I think I'll wear this confidence every day, it's a good fit
Some days, I might be a little down,
But I can change that, turn that frown upside down.

MAHI PANDYA

CROWD

Bodies of people I love surround me,
Then why can't I just let loose, be free?
There's a sword hanging over my head,
Trust issues, got me weak, they want me dead.

They crowd over me, wait for me to fall,
And when they need something it's my name they call.
They say you're ignoring us they say I'm cold hearted,
I want to know when this will end when I didn't even start it.

I wanna lock myself in the closet,
I don't want to answer them when they ask if I'm upset.
Cause " loved ones" will know how I'm feeling,
Instead of laughing at me they should help my healing.

But humans are social animals, can't live without contact,
It's time I set we an example, change that fact.
It's time I find a room to breathe and room to grow,
Away from the crowd and away from the show.

MAHI PANDYA

LAYERS

This is so new, yet I've known it for so long
life's like the reruns of the same song
Isn't it nice to be stuck here, to be neutral
then why does this feel like a funeral

I fear I don't know who I am anymore
I've been knocking but can't find out what's
behind that door
Maybe I've wrung the last drop of life out
My eyes are dry, throat too parched to shout

I heard it in a song, it told me to hang on
I'm finding that energy, that God I used to pray upon
I've waited too long, now I'm sending for help SOS
Don't want to call the undertaker, he can clean up this mess

For too long I've felt this way, no one saw
I'm too conceited, I'm not good at being raw
I asked for happiness in my prayers,
Today I stripped down to my insecurities,
I threw away my layers

MAHI PANDYA

ANGER

All this arguing and I chose to be quiet
I'm the victim here but I still let you be right
I wait for you to leave, like everyone
I decided a long time ago that I'm done

I'm not good at giving you a piece of my mind
I tell myself I'm taking the high road, I'm being kind
But my patience is hanging on by a thread
And if I shut you out, you can't mess with my head

I don't really know when was the last time we were happy
I smile and laugh but my mood is snappy
I thought I was done with the bullies and
then you came around
I don't know who hurt you but you're meaner
than you sound

They say let it out, you have to shout
I want to, but my words Won't Leave my mouth
I've kept all this anger down, I keep it light
But you can see it now, through whatever I write

MAHI PANDYA

PASSIVE AGGRESSIVE ATTACK

We all hope for love, hope for serenity,
You keep your pride, I keep my dignity.
But would it hurt for you to say a thank you,
Gratitude for me being alive, for all I do.

Push past the gratitude, let's talk about appreciation,
What does one get for being loyal, for one's dedication.
Nothing's permanent, I know that,
Let me just rewind and recheck that fact.

Because I'll take your words to the grave,
I will remember the memories of you I save.
How you put me down when I needed you the most,
You're the parasite and I'm the host.

But this, not a passive-aggressive attack,
It's to openly remind myself of what you lack.
It's the compassion that humanity is made of,
I just hope you are something you're proud of.

MAHI PANDYA

www.ingramcontent.com/pod-product-compliance
Ingram Content Group UK Ltd.
Pitfield, Milton Keynes, MK11 3LW, UK
UKHW040003200726
13854UKWH00001B/21

9 789387 131309